And
Goes To The
Aquarium

Nick & Pierce Marrs

illustrations, cover & book design: Rose Gauss

4mpress ❖ Thompsons Station, Tennessee ❖ ©2013

Nick and Pierce are a father and son team from a small town outside of Nashville, TN. They are accomplished writers, speakers, and possess a strong desire to serve. Nick published his first book, **Simple, But Not Easy** in the spring of 2013 and Pierce's debut book **Sharing Enthusiasm** is due to be released in the fall of 2013. Nick is also a personal trainer and Pierce is a highly sought after sales and life coach. Their shared passion for family, along with their own dynamics and life lessons has been the basis for **Andy's Adventure Series**. Pierce is the father of Nick and his younger brother Nathan, and has been married to their mom Lesa for twenty-nine years. Nick married his wife Darci in the fall of 2012.

Besides working with traditional publishers Rose Gauss has done illustration & design work for several self-published book authors. She has also written and illustrated her own children's books, including **The Draw Book**. Rose & her husband live outside Pittsburgh, Pennsylvanina in an old farm house and have three grown children and two grandchildren. You can visit her web site: **theDRAWpage.com** for lots of fun drawing & coloring activities.

Published by: 4mpress www.4mpress.com Thompsons Station, Tennessee

The illustrations were rendered in pen & ink and watercolor
and enhanced in Photoshop. www.RoseGauss.com
The font is: Noteworthy Light

"We dedicate this book to...our family."
Nick &
Pierce

Today is Andy's birthday.
He likes all the presents,
but he loves to
blow out the candles.

This is when he gets to
make his birthday wish.

Andy wishes for the same thing
every year, he wants a best friend.

"My brothers all have best friends, why not me?" Andy wonders.

On the last day of school Andy is excited because summer is his favorite time of year. He hopes this time his birthday wish will come true, and he will find his best friend.

The next day
Andy's mom
surprises them
with a trip to
the aquarium.

Andy is very
excited,
he has never
been to an
aquarium!

AQUARIUM
TICKETS

AQUARIUM
TICKETS

AQUARIUM
TICKETS

AQUARIUM
TICKETS

s add fees
axes

Admit One
9am to 6pm
hout the year
e visitor.

pm
e year
isitor.

year
or.

the year
isitor.

ticket
RESALE
one visitor

Andy's older brothers are allowed
to bring their best friends.

This makes Andy feel lonely
because he doesn't have
a best friend to invite.

When they arrive, Andy can't
wait to see all the animals.
...the fish...the sharks...the turtles...

He wonders what else
he will see
at the aquarium.

Once inside Andy exclaims,
"I didn't know there would be penguins!
Can we go see them now, Mom?"

"Soon!" said his mother with a smile.

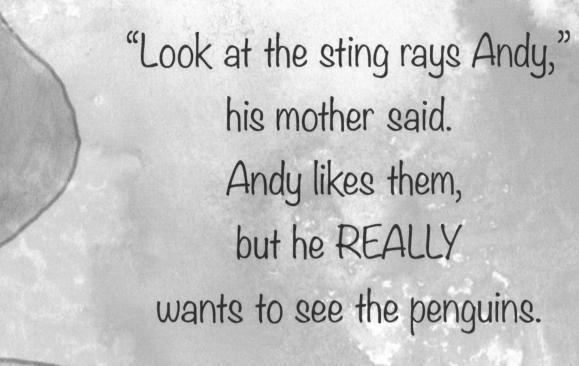

"Look at the sting rays Andy,"
his mother said.
Andy likes them,
but he REALLY
wants to see the penguins.

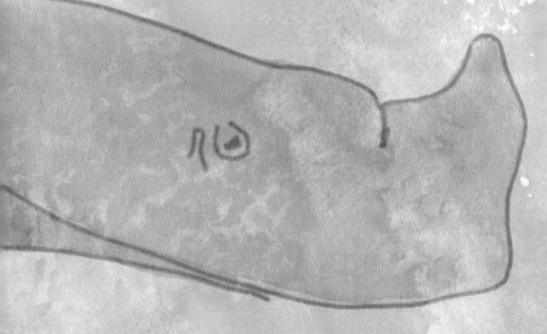

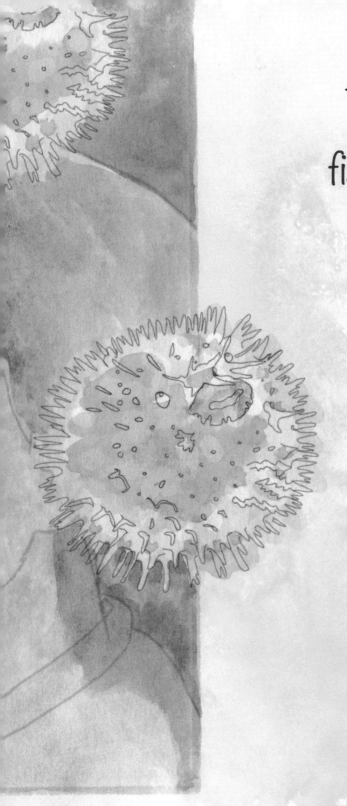

The boys make
fishy faces at the
blowfish
through the
glass.

Andy laughs,
but he still
wants to find
the penguins.

SHARKS

Mother asks,
"What do you think
of the sharks Andy?"

PENGUINS

But he doesn't answer because he's not with his family anymore. Andy is missing!

Andy's family looks all over for him, but they can't find him anywhere.

"Where would he have gone?" says his worried father.

Andy has finally
found the penguins!

"The small one
looks lonely
like me,"
he thinks to
himself.
"Maybe he
needs
a best
friend too."

"How did you get in there?"
exclaims the security guard.

Then he takes Andy
to look for his family.

Andy's mother
is happy to
find him
and
surprised
to see him
so messy.

"We were
worried
about you!"

"Why did you wander off?"
his mother asks.

"I was looking for the penguins,"
he said.
"The little penguin was
all by himself
and looked lonely, like me.
I wanted to be
his friend."

On the way home
Andy mutters,
"Mom, I've got one."

"What do you mean
you've got one ?"
Mom asks.

"I mean...
I've got one...
in my backpack,"
Andy said quietly.

"He looked so lonely,
I brought him with me to
be my friend," Andy said
with a smile.

"Oh no!"
His mother said
"We have to turn
around and take him back!
He belongs at the aquarium
with his family."

Andy apologized,
"I'm sorry for taking your penguin."

The aquarium manager replied,
"Thank you for bringing him back home."

She went on to explain
how important it was
for the penguin to stay
with his own family.
"Since you were so honest,
we have a little surprise for you."

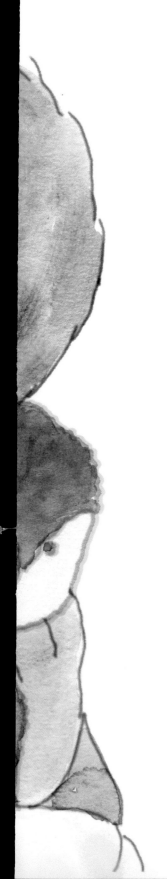

"Here you go Andy, your
very own penguin to take
home with you."
The manager said as she gave
him his new toy.

He loved his new stuffed
animal friend,
but was still sad to leave
the real penguin behind.

"Andy, what did you learn today?"
his father asked.

"I shouldn't take things that don't belong to me," Andy said, "And never go off by myself without telling my parents first."

"That's right. We were very worried, but glad that you're okay. Let's go home," his father said.

"Hey Andy, are you okay?"
his brother asked.

"I miss my friend"
Andy sighed.

His brother said,
"We can be your
best friends
from now on."

This made
Andy happy.

Even though Andy wished for
his own best friend every year,

he found out that his real best friends were his family all along.

CPSIA information can be obtained
at www.ICGtesting.com
Printed in the USA
LVIC04n2309161013
357306LV00001B/1